IGGY
RULES THE
ANIMAL
KINGDOM

Look for all of Iggy's triumphs

IGGY

RULES THE ANIMAL KINGDOM

ANNIE BARROWS

ILLUSTRATED BY SAM RICKS

putnam

G. P. Putnam's Sons

G. P. PUTNAM'S SONS
An imprint of Penguin Random House LLC, New York

First published in the United States of America by G. P. Putnam's Sons,
an imprint of Penguin Random House LLC, 2023

Text copyright © 2023 by Annie Barrows
Illustrations copyright © 2023 by Sam Ricks

G. P. Putnam's Sons is a registered trademark of Penguin Random House LLC.
Penguin Books and colophon are registered trademarks of Penguin Books Limited.

Visit us online at penguinrandomhouse.com.

Library of Congress Cataloging-in-Publication Data is available.

Printed in the United States of America

ISBN 9780593325377 (library binding)

ISBN 9780593325384 (paperback)
1st Printing

LSCC

Design by Marikka Tamura and Cindy De la Cruz
Text set in New Century Schoolbook LT Std.

CONTENTS

CHAPTER 1

MATURITY: A BAD IDEA

Grown-ups are funny people.

Irrational.

Illogical.

Immitrical (okay, okay, that's not a real word, but it sounds good with the other two).

Grown-ups actually make no sense at all.

Take, for example, babies. Grown-ups *love* babies! They love babies even though they're little, bald, useless lumps. In fact, they love them *because* they're little, bald, useless lumps. Grown-ups cuddle them and feed them and rock them. They even clean up their poopy diapers.

Do grown-ups say to babies, "We've been thinking, and it's time you demonstrated more sense of responsibility"?

No.

Do they say to babies, "We expect more mature behavior"?

No.

Babies are just about the most immature and irresponsible people on earth, and grown-ups are crazy about them.

So why, when you turn eight or nine or ten or eleven, do maturity and responsibility suddenly become your grown-ups' favorite things ever? Here you were, thinking your grown-ups *liked* immature, irresponsible behavior—and now, without warning, you start to get in trouble for it.

This is unfair. This is changing the rules in the middle of the game, also called "moving the goalposts," which is just a nice way to say cheating, because even I could make a goal if I moved the goalpost right next to my foot.

Besides—you shouldn't have to tell your grown-ups this, but apparently you do—you are, after all, just a kid. You're not old enough to be mature!

And furthermore, would they really like it if you *were* mature? If you started sighing and talking about traffic and complaining about your back and your hair, would your grown-ups be happy?

Do you think it would look better if I dyed it?

Which brings up another point: If grown-ups are so fired up about maturity, why are they always complaining about being old? They don't make it sound like much fun. They should think about this.

So I'll tell you about my back. It all began one day when I was twenty-seven— No! Wait! I must have been twenty-eight because that was the year I started to like tea . . .

What? What? Speak up!

We are not going to think about it, because we have some other stuff to do. Specifically, we are going to learn about a surprising thing that happened to Iggy Frangi.

Who is Iggy Frangi, you ask?

Really?

You haven't read the other books about him? Sheesh.

Iggy Frangi is a kid. He's nine years old. What more do you need to know?

Okay, fine! Here's some more: Iggy Frangi is generous, hardworking, brave, resourceful, and caring. He has tried to protect his family from crime, even though they didn't appreciate it. He has tried to help others, especially with their teeth. He has taught people things they never knew before, mostly about gardening supplies.* Yes, Iggy Frangi is an inspiration to those around him!

Which makes it all the more surprising that Iggy's mom and dad ever wanted him to be different. But they did.

---

*If you had read the other books, you would know all this. Just saying.

4

CHAPTER 2

IGGY'S (NONEXISTENT) PUPPY

In order for you to understand why Iggy's mom and dad surprisingly wanted him to be different, you need to know something about Iggy. It's not a surprising thing. It's a completely normal and reasonable thing.

Iggy wanted a puppy.

Iggy had always wanted a puppy. As far back as he could remember, he'd wanted a puppy.

In Iggy's opinion, he was the kind of kid who was *supposed* to have a puppy. He knew how happy he'd be—all the time—if he had a puppy. On sunny days, he and the puppy would go to the park; he'd throw the ball, and the puppy would chase it.

On cold nights, the puppy would sleep next to him, and they'd both be warm. When Iggy had homework, his puppy would sit next to his desk, lifting his head to give Iggy a sympathetic look every now and then. When Iggy's friends came over, they'd want to play with the puppy because the puppy was so much fun, but in the end,

the puppy would trot back to
Iggy, because he'd always love
Iggy the best.

Iggy didn't even care what kind of puppy it was, that's how much he wanted one. Big or small, didn't matter—though it couldn't be one of those teeny-weeny ones that quivered. Long hair or short, didn't matter—though it couldn't be one of those goofy ones with puffy balls of fuzz on its ankles. It didn't even have to be a puppy! It could be a grown-up dog—though it couldn't be one of those gross ones with crusty eyes.

You are probably asking why, if Iggy wanted a puppy so much, he had no puppy.

Iggy had asked that very question.

In fact, he had asked his parents that very question about five hundred times. Why did he ask the same question five hundred times? Did he forget the answer? No, he didn't. He was just hoping the answer would change.

Actually, his parents gave him lots of different answers. Here's one:

Oh, Iggy, we have too much going on around here to get a dog!

(Iggy looked around the house
and saw nothing going on.
That's why he wanted a dog.)

Here's another:

> Nobody has time to
> take care of a dog.

(Iggy did!)

Or:

> This place is already
> a mess, and a dog would
> make it worse.

(What mess? There was no mess.)

And then, the tough one,
the big one, the one that Iggy
couldn't deny or fight or solve:

> Dogs make your
> dad sneeze.

What could Iggy say
to that? "Let's get rid of
Dad"? Of course not! Dad was
great! (Except for the sneezing.)

So the years went on, and Iggy remained puppyless.

• • •

Then came a certain Sunday afternoon in March. You know how Sunday afternoons are, right? Long. All the weekend fun you were looking forward to is over, and tomorrow is Monday and school and the regular boring, hard things. Nothing is fun enough on a Sunday afternoon.

This certain Sunday afternoon was no different. Iggy was bored. He was bored and he was mad about being bored, because it was the weekend, and he should have been having fun, not slomping around.

First, he slomped around in his room.

Then, he slomped around in the front yard.

Finally, he slomped around in the back yard. He boinged on the trampoline. He threw a tennis ball at the back of the garage. He lifted one of the paving stones to see if there was a snake under it (nope). He pulled his shirt up over his head and staggered around, just in case he ever had to escape from his back yard blindfolded. He crashed into the shed. It didn't hurt much, but he fell over anyway, because maybe someone was watching, someone who would rush outside and say, "Are you all right?! Do you need some candy?"

Nobody rushed outside. Iggy got up. He looked at the shed. He hadn't been inside the shed for a while. He had almost forgotten what was in there. Maybe there was something good! Like money! Or a sword! Or the Krazy Glue, which had disappeared from the tool drawer after Iggy used it.*

*We are not going to discuss this event.

Slomping no more, Iggy opened the door of the shed, dived in, and— Uck! He spat out a mouthful of spiderwebs. Then he began to search among the bicycles and camping gear. A sword is pretty big, but money and Krazy Glue aren't, so he had to look inside all the backpacks. He found a toothpick. He found a flashlight and flicked it on. There! Now he could see all the money that had been tucked into backpack pockets. There wasn't any. Not even a quarter. No Krazy Glue either.

Did Iggy give up? No! Iggy stuck to it! He shoved his way through the bicycles—ouch—until he got behind them, where there was a metal cupboard, the perfect place to hide a sword! He flung open the doors and found—tin cans. A first aid kit. A rope. A bunch of flowerpots.

Boring.

Iggy decided to go back to slomping. But as he was turning to leave, his flashlight beamed on a mysterious object in the farthest corner of the shed. He peered at it. He peered some more.

It looked like a—

But how could it be?

It couldn't—

But it was!

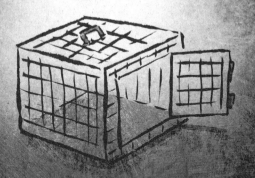

It was a dog-training crate.

Just in case you don't know what that is: A dog-training crate is a big plastic or wire box you put puppies in to teach them not to wake up in the middle of the night and howl.

Iggy knew what it was. He had seen a training crate in a book he had checked out of the library called *You and Your Puppy*. He had selected this book in order to read it in front of his mom and dad, sighing heavily. This had not resulted in a puppy, but it had resulted in his parents repeating all the reasons why he couldn't get one.

Iggy draped himself over the metal cupboard and stretched his arms as far as they would go.

Grunting, he lifted the crate out from behind the cupboard. Yes. It was a dog-training crate. It was old and dusty, but it was unmistakably a dog-training crate.

Why would Iggy's parents have a dog-training crate in their shed? They'd never had a dog. Dogs made Iggy's dad sneeze.

They said.

Iggy looked at the dog-training crate in his hands, and a shocking thought arose in his mind.

Maybe, just maybe, his parents had *lied*.

CHAPTER 3

PANTS ON FIRE

It was a pretty big dog-training crate. It was so big it covered most of Iggy's face as he carried it across the back yard, up the stairs to the deck, between the deck chairs, and in the back door. So it was no wonder he didn't see his mom when he came into the kitchen. She really should have been paying more attention.

"OW!" she squawked. "That was my *leg*, Iggy! Watch where you're going with that— that . . . Where did you find *that*?"

"In the back of the shed," said Iggy.

"It's filthy dirty," she said, brushing off her pants. "You can just take it right back outside."

Iggy did not take it right back outside. Instead, he set it on the floor and asked, "What is it?"

His mom hesitated. "I have no idea."

Iggy looked at her with squinty eyes. "It's a dog-training crate."

"Is that right?" she asked, which, if you think about it, doesn't mean anything. "I wonder what it was doing in our shed."

"That's what I want to know!" said Iggy squintily. "What's a dog-training crate doing in our shed?"

Unlike Iggy's, his mom's eyes were getting rounder and rounder. "I have no idea."

At this different-eye-size moment, Iggy's older sister, Maribel, breezed into the kitchen with a pencil behind her ear. "I *really* need to invite Tiegen to my slumber party, Mom."

"Let's discuss it!" said Iggy's mom, whirling around as if she was extremely happy to stop talking about dog-training crates.

"Aw, look," said Maribel, catching sight of Iggy and his crate. "It's Chessy's box. I remember that."

There was another moment, this one of silence. During it, Iggy's mom winced.

"Chessy WHO?" Iggy yelled.

"Oops." Maribel giggled. "Sorry, Mom."

"Oops *what*?" squawked Iggy. "Chessy *who*?"

"I'm not supposed to tell you," said Maribel.

"Go ahead," Mom sighed.

"Chessy the dog," said Maribel. "His whole name was Chessy Chessburger, right, Mom? I can't believe I remember that!"

"CHESSY THE DOG?" bellowed Iggy.

"YOU HAD A DOG? YOU SAID WE COULDN'T HAVE A DOG BECAUSE OF DAD! YOU LIED!"

"Well . . ." said Iggy's mom.

"We had him until you were about one," said Maribel. "Then he bit you, so they gave him away. I wanted Mom and Dad to give you away, but they wouldn't. Right, Mom?" She laughed.

Iggy didn't. Iggy glared at his mom and said, "Give me one good reason why I can't have a puppy."

Iggy's parents, filled with shame, said, "Oh, Iggy, we don't know what we were thinking! We lied! We feel terrible! We will jump in the car and go to the animal shelter and get you a puppy right this second if you will forgive us for lying! We're sorry!"

Iggy said, "Okay. But don't do it again."

Then they went to the animal shelter, and Iggy found the puppy he had always dreamed of. He brought it home and named it Popcorn, and they lived happily ever after, except for Iggy's parents, who still felt bad about lying. As they should.

WHAT DID HAPPEN NEXT

An amazingly long conversation that—you're not going to believe this, but it's true—did *not* consist of Iggy's parents apologizing. Oh, sure, they said they were sorry, but it was like this: "We're sorry that we misled you, but that doesn't change our opinion, which is that you are not mature enough to handle the responsibility of a dog."

After that, there was a lot of blabbering about what *mature* and *responsible* meant.

After that, a list was made. It was called "Ways to Show Maturity and Responsibility."

After that, promises were made.

After that, there were glances between his parents. There was a nod.

And in the end, which was two hours later, Iggy did not have a puppy, but he did have a deal.

If he could prove to his parents that he was mature and responsible, they would get him a puppy.

CHAPTER 4

THE
SUNDAY AFTERNOON
OF A
MATURE PERSON

As you know, Sunday afternoons go on forever, so even after the amazingly long conversation, Iggy still had time to begin being mature and responsible. He looked down at the list his mom had written for him.

WAYS TO SHOW MATURITY
AND RESPONSIBILITY

1. Clean your room.

2. Help around the house.

3. Be nice to your sisters.

4. Take care of yourself,
   your stuff, and your
   obligations* without
   having to be reminded.

Obligations means "things you're supposed to do."
Secretly, it also means "things you don't want to do."

Hmm. Apparently, *maturity* and *responsibility* mean the same thing as *boring* and *annoying*.

But okay! No problem! Iggy would show them! He decided to start by cleaning his room. It looked fine to him, but he'd clean it anyway.

He pulled the bedspread up nice and neat. He picked up a shirt from the floor and almost put it in his drawer until he thought, What if I want to wear it tomorrow? Any mature person would agree that it was dumb to put it away if he might want to wear it tomorrow. He put it back on the floor, but folded.

He looked around again, trying to find something else to clean. He put some of his old (certainly not currently-played-with) action figures in a straight line on his desk.

He put his homework folder inside his backpack, which was—(ew, yuck)—filled with crumbs and balled-up plastic wrap, but his backpack obviously was not his room, so there was no need to clean it.

Okay! He had cleaned his room!

He put a check mark beside #1 on his list. He felt great! This must be how mature people feel all the time, he thought. "Good job!" he said to

himself in the mirror. While he was there, he practiced making mature faces. Like this:

He noticed that he didn't look very mature. He stared at himself. It was his hair. Mature people have neat hair. Iggy's hair was the opposite of neat. It looked like sticks poking out of the ground. Maybe he could fix it, though. And maybe if he fixed it, he would *look* so mature that his parents would be fooled and he wouldn't have to do any of the boring other things on the list.

It was worth a try.

Iggy went in the bathroom and spent several minutes trying to pull a comb through his hair. No dice.

Maybe if he got it wet first.

Nope. He spent several minutes trying to pull the comb through his wet hair. Then he spent several minutes trying to pull the comb out of his wet hair.

Ouch.

"Dinner!" his dad yelled from downstairs.

"Coming!" Iggy yelled.

But he wasn't; he was rooting around in Maribel's shelf of lotions and brushes and bands. She put some kind of goo in her hair to make it smooth— what was it called? Oh! Here! He yanked out the bottle. Strawberry Softie Anti-Frizz Style Pudding! Exactly what he needed. And it was a huge bottle too. She'd never notice, because all he needed was a tiny bit anyway, just a little—

Oops.

Iggy tried to wash some off.

Oops. The sink.

29

Iggy tried to wipe the sink.

Oops. The towel.

Maybe once he put it in his hair, it would get smaller.

Maybe he needed to rub it around.

It didn't move. It stayed right where he'd dropped it. Those hairs definitely looked neater. The rest of his head looked pretty much the same.

"Dinner *now*, Iggy!" bellowed his dad.

Iggy bolted downstairs and skidded into the dining room.

"Lookit!" cried his little sister, Molly. "Iggy got clown hair!"

CHAPTER 5

THE
SUNDAY EVENING
OF A
MATURE PERSON

Was not so good.

CHAPTER 6

THE NEW LEAF

Iggy realized he hadn't gotten off to the best start. He realized it, and he resolved to turn over a new leaf. He reviewed his list. He made a plan. Maturity was just around the corner!

So the next morning, when Iggy's dad stuck his head in Iggy's room and said, "Time to get up, son," Iggy did it! (This was #4: Take care of yourself, your stuff, and your obligations.)

Iggy washed his face! (Also #4.)

Iggy ate his breakfast and did not complain about school! (This was basically #2: Help around the house.)

Iggy carried his bowl to the sink! (*Totally* #2.)

Iggy did not yell "Where's my backpack?! Someone took it!" or "I can't find my jacket!" (#4.)

Iggy did not make fun of Maribel's shirt! (#3: Be nice to your sisters.)

Iggy did not tell Molly that he'd heard her preschool had burned down over the weekend! (Same.)

Iggy brushed his teeth! (#4.)

When Iggy's mom kissed him good-bye, Iggy

did not slap his cheek and run away! He said, "Bye, Mom." Then he added, "Have a good day." (This was not even on the list. This was extra!)

Unbelievably, no one seemed to notice.

Maybe they were just tired, thought Iggy as he walked to school. He was tired too. It was exhausting, being so mature. For once, he was looking forward to school, because at school, no one expected him to be mature. He could just be regular. He needed a few hours of vacation before it was time to go home and start being mature again.

This puppy had better love him a lot.

CHAPTER 7

IGGY IS MATURE
AND RESPONSIBLE,
AND
THERE IS YELLING
ANYWAY

At school, Iggy rested. He rested by pretending he was going to put Arden's pencil case in the snake tank and then by giving Donal thirty-five cents to turn his eyelid inside out (gross!) and then by trying to climb on the roof of the sports shed (after that one, he had to rest on the bench for a while) and then by singing "BABY SHARK DO DO DO" at the top of his lungs during PE.

"What's gotten into you today, Iggy?" asked his teacher, Ms. Schulberger.

And it was lucky Iggy had rested so much at school, because the minute he got home, he had to be mature again. And not just mature—responsible too.

"Oh, Iggy, I'm so glad you're here!" his mom said when he walked in the front door. Iggy thought she was happy to see him because he had been so nice that morning. But that wasn't it. "I forgot Molly's school ended early today, and now she's home, and I've just *got* to go into a video meeting, so can you watch her for about—oh, I don't know!—twenty minutes? Oh gosh, it starts in two minutes! How's my hair?" She looked at him questioningly.

"Brown," said Iggy.

"Iggy, come take care of me!" shouted Molly from the family room.

"Gotta go!" cried his mom, rushing to the computer room.

"This is two, three, and four!" Iggy pointed out, but she didn't seem to hear.

"Iggy!" screeched Molly.

• • •

Iggy's little sister, Molly, was three years old. Her most favorite thing was drawing, so when Iggy went into the family room, he figured Molly would draw and he would take the opportunity to check out ESPN on his Dad's laptop.

Unfortunately, Molly's second most favorite thing was ordering people around. "You, Iggy, you draw me," she said. "Sit here." She pointed to the puny chair that went with her puny art table.

Remembering #3, Iggy squished himself into the chair. "Okay."

"Now," began Molly, handing him a piece of paper. "Draw me. No, not with green. Stop it. With purple and pink. Not that purple. Stop it. You wasted paper. Here's a new one. Now, make me wearing a crown. No! You have to draw the hair! That's not how it looks! Stop it! Do it again!"

Iggy crumpled up the paper and got a new one. "Hey, you can't tell other people how to draw."

"I'm not telling." She stuck out her tongue at him. "Draw me better."

Iggy drew her with her tongue out.

"No!" she yelled. "Bad Iggy! You make me better!!"

"That's how you look, shorty." Iggy laughed (momentarily forgetting about #3). "I can't help it if you're weird-looking."

"I not short! I not weird! *You* weird! You ugly and flecked!" yelled Molly (she meant "freckled"). She snatched the paper out from under Iggy's marker, causing him to draw a line on the table.

"Molly!" groaned Iggy. "Look what you did."

"You! You did it!"

"But it's your fault, so you have to clean it up," Iggy said (momentarily forgetting about #4) (and possibly #2).

Molly glared at him. "No."

"Fine," said Iggy. "I'll tell Mom you drew on the table."

Molly's face turned the color of a pomegranate. "Big ugly liar Iggy!" she shouted. "You BIG UGGY IGGY!"

"Shh! Hush up!" Iggy hissed, anxiously looking at the door. If his mom heard Molly shouting, she was going to have to leave in the middle of her video meeting, and he was going to get no credit at all for being mature and responsible. "Just shut up for once in your life."

Uh-oh.

Molly opened her mouth as wide as it would go, and Iggy knew exactly what was going to happen next.

She was
going to scream
as loud as she could.
Which was amazingly
loud. And then his mom was
going to come rushing down
the hall. And then *he* was
going to get in trouble.
Big, puppy-ending
trouble.

There was only one way out.

So Iggy took it.

• • •

When Iggy's mom was finished with her meeting, she emerged to a peaceful home. No one was crying. The family room was not wrecked. The kitchen wasn't covered in crumbs or smears. No screams or shrieks were heard.

All was quiet. Calm.

Her hardworking son was bent over his math homework, a healthful snack of apple half-eaten beside him.

And her younger daughter was . . . well, she was having fun. Good, clean, outdoor fun.

Really, what more could a mother ask?

I am sorry to report that Iggy's mother *did* ask. She looked around the room, frowned, and asked, "Where's Molly?"

"Outside," said Iggy. "In the back yard."

His mom frowned harder. "Outside? By herself? Iggy! That's not okay!"

He looked up. "She's fine. She's totally safe."

His mom didn't answer because she was racing out the back door.

WHAT SHOULD HAVE HAPPENED NEXT

A few moments later, Iggy's mom returned. "Wow," she said. "Good job keeping your sister safe and happy. Even Maribel can't do that."

"It was easy," said Iggy. "Next time you need help, just let me know," he added, because he was the kind of kid who helps around the house.

His mom smiled at him lovingly. "Thanks, sweetie. But you won't be able to put her in the dog crate again."

"Why not?" asked Iggy innocently.

"Because I think there's going to be a puppy in there," she said, and then they hugged each other and went to the animal shelter to get Iggy's brand-new puppy, while Molly played happily in the back yard.

 ## WHAT DID HAPPEN NEXT

Apparently, you are not supposed to stuff your little sister in a dog-training crate. Even if she likes it. Even if she's playing puppy and having a great time, you're not supposed to do it. Even if she is perfectly safe—*more* safe than she would be inside the house, where there are scissors and pins—you are still not supposed to do it.

And get this! It is apparently *especially* mean to lock the crate once she's in there, even though that's why she's safe. As well as being very bad, for some unknown reason, to leave her outside in the crate, barking and yapping, and return indoors yourself, even though you are maturely and responsibly doing your math homework, which you certainly couldn't do outside with all that noise going on.

Well. Life is full of surprising discoveries.

Iggy's life was particularly full of surprising discoveries, but they weren't the happy kind. They were the kind where you found out that your behavior was "not at all what I expect from you," your mom was "very disappointed in you," and "if you think that's being mature and responsible, you have a very long way to go before you're ready to take care of a dog."

CHAPTER 8

THE OLD, SHRIVELED LEAF

By Thursday morning, Iggy was discouraged. If you ignored the events of Sunday evening and Monday afternoon, that still meant he had been good for a total of two and a half days, which should have canceled out Monday afternoon (when, in his opinion, he had been *fine*) and Sunday evening (which was a minor problem that didn't hurt anyone, and he was the one who had to take an extra shower and clean up the bathroom, so what were they upset about?). Otherwise, he had been *amazing*.

He had been so mature and responsible, he was practically a forty-year-old. Not once had he been late. Not once had he complained. He had done all his chores. He had been kind. He had been so kind, he carried a bag of groceries into the house without being asked! So kind, he'd helped Maribel carry the inflatable mattress up from the basement for her slumber party! So kind, he'd asked his mom if she needed any help with dinner! And then he had peeled carrots!

"I finished the carrots," he announced.

His mom turned around. "Well, Iggy," she said, smiling, "that was the final test, and you passed it with flying colors! Tomorrow after school, we'll go to the animal shelter, and you can pick out your puppy!"

 WHAT DID HAPPEN NEXT

His mom said, "Great, thanks. Will you put them in that bowl over there?"

• • •

Is it any wonder that by Thursday morning, Iggy arrived in Ms. Schulberger's fourth-grade classroom in a state of discouragement? Soon, however, his mood improved.

It began improving when Sarah tripped over her own feet. It improved more when Iggy got his spelling test back and he did way better than his buddy Arch. But it improved most of all when Ms. Schulberger announced that their classroom was scheduled for a deep clean that weekend and she happened to be going out of town, so the class pets needed homes to go to.

Iggy straightened up in his chair. This was it! This was his big opportunity! "ME!" yelled Iggy, his hand shooting in the air. "I'll take 'em. I'll take 'em all!"

What could be a better way to demonstrate that he could take care of a puppy than taking care of a hamster, a chinchilla, and a snake all at once?

There was a little arguing from Arden, who wanted the hamster but admitted in the end that her four cats would probably eat him, and from Aidan, who wanted the snake but admitted in the end that he just wanted to wear it around his neck, not take care of it.

"I'll take care of them!" said Iggy loudly. "I'll even clean their cages!"

"Are you sure this is going to be okay with your parents?" asked Ms. Schulberger anxiously.

"My parents?" said Iggy. "They're crazy about animals! We're going to get a puppy pretty soon!" (True!)

"Okay. Great. But why don't you check in with them tonight?" suggested Ms. Schulberger. "Just to be sure."

Iggy said he would.

He meant it too. But unfortunately, he forgot.

CHAPTER 9

PANCAKE, GARY, AND MR. LURCH

In fact, Iggy forgot all about hamsters, chin-chillas, and snakes until the next day when he arrived at Ms. Schulberger's classroom, freshly exhausted from a morning of maturity. That particular morning had taken a lot out of him.

Not *only* had he taken his cereal bowl to the sink after he was done eating, but when Maribel came downstairs wearing purple hair chalk, he had *not* said "Did something die on your head?" And when she said, "Tonight at my slumber party, we're going to do makeovers!" Iggy did *not* say "It's going to take more than one night to make you over." And when she said, "Don't be thinking you can come to my party, Iggy. You have to stay in your room and not bug us," Iggy did *not* say "You think I want to see your dweeby friends? No thanks!"

He just nodded maturely, being nice to his sister (#3).

Did anyone appreciate this mature (and exhausting) niceness? No. His mom turned and gave him a (completely undeserved) stern look. "That's right, Iggy. You need to leave the girls alone to have their own fun. It's really important to Maribel to have a nice party."

"You can have a piece of cake," said Maribel. "As long as you eat it in your room."

Iggy did *not* say "I don't even want your gross cake." (Because he did want it.) He just nodded.

But, boy, was it tough, holding all those words inside. Iggy was worn to a nubbin by the time he got to school.

• • •

Ms. Schulberger was Iggy's favorite teacher ever. She was nice and pretty and young, and best of all, she never got mad at Iggy. All his other teachers had gotten mad at him. Some of them were *still* mad.* Not Ms. Schulberger. Every morning, she said "Iggy!" and smiled at him. Even when Iggy did something like pretend his binder was eating his head, she didn't get mad. She just said "That's enough of that, Iggy."

Another good thing about Ms. Schulberger was animals. She loved them. She didn't just love cute animals. She also loved animals like hyenas that nobody else even liked. When she showed her students what research notes were, her notes were about moths and butterflies. In math, her Venn diagrams were about apes and monkeys. Read-aloud was almost always a book about animals. And while other classrooms had *maybe* one guinea pig, Ms. Schulberger's classroom had a hamster named Pancake, a chinchilla named Gary, and a corn snake named Mr. Lurch.

---

*Hi, Ms. Dixson!

55

So when Iggy arrived at Ms. Schulberger's classroom on Friday morning, an old, shriveled, unappreciated leaf, and Ms. Schulberger smiled at him and said, "Iggy! Did your folks say it was okay to take Pancake, Gary, and Mr. Lurch this weekend?"—what do you think he said?

. . .

Exactly right! Iggy said, "Yes. They said it was fine."

Ms. Schulberger let out a breath. "What a relief! They completely sprung the deep clean on me, and I don't know *what* I would have done if you couldn't take them. I'm so glad it worked out, Iggy. Thank you!" She smiled gratefully.

And that is why, at 3:12 that afternoon, Iggy found himself standing on the sidewalk in front of his school with a large plastic case containing a snake, a small plastic-and-wire case containing

a hamster, and a complicated plastic-and-wire cage containing a chinchilla.

He didn't know what to do.

How was he going to get home?

Maybe he'd just stand there forever.

Maybe he'd run away to Ketchum, Idaho.

No, he couldn't run away to Ketchum, Idaho, carrying a snake, a hamster, and a chinchilla. Ms. Schulberger was counting on him. She had given him typed instructions and bags of food, which he was also carrying.

How was he going to get home?

He knew the answer: He was going to have to call his mom. She'd be mad. His dad would be mad too. They would use the words *immature* and *irresponsible*. And then Iggy wouldn't get a puppy. He would have nothing to show for all those chores and held-in words. It was a terrible thought.

"*Weep!*" said Gary the chinchilla.

How true, thought Iggy sadly.

"Whatcha doing, Iggy?" It was his buddy Arch, calling out the window of his mom's van. *His mom's van!*

"Arch!" hollered Iggy. "Arch! Can I have a ride home? Hi, Mrs. Parris! Can I please have a ride home? Please?"

Arch's mom leaned forward to peer out the window. "Wow. It sure looks like you could use one, Iggy. Let me pull over."

Iggy said "Thanks!" and "Sorry!" about forty times while he loaded the cages into the car. He said them another seventy times during the five-minute drive. And maybe fifteen more times while unloading the cages. "Thank you!" he shouted as Arch and his mom pulled away. "Sorry! Thanks for the ride!" He waved at the back of the car. "See you! Sorry! Thanks!" He waved until the car disappeared around the corner.

"Weep!" said Gary, rocketing up and down his little ramps.

Well, right.

Because even though the good news was, he wasn't going to have to stand out in front of the school all weekend, the bad news was, everything else was just the same. Mad mom, mad dad, no puppy, wasted maturity. Iggy sighed. He might as well get it over with. He turned toward the house.

This was when he noticed that his mom's car wasn't in the driveway.

His mom's car wasn't in the driveway! This meant something important: *His mom wasn't home!*

Seeing this, an amazing idea burst to life in Iggy's mind. A brilliant idea! An idea that would result in Gary, Pancake, and Mr. Lurch being well cared for; his mom and dad being impressed; and Iggy being a person with a puppy! Wow! Total happiness was within his grasp!

But Iggy couldn't just stand there admiring his idea. No, he had to move and move fast! Because unless he got Gary, Mr. Lurch, and Pancake into his room without anybody seeing, his idea was ruined.

CHAPTER 10

WHAT GARY THOUGHT

Earthquake! Earthquake! *Run!*

Oh. Not an earthquake. A loud, bony human.

Get away, human!

I am **Gary the Chinchilla**. You dare to tip my house?! I will chew you!

Tip! He did it again. Tip! I will go mad! Where is the quiet, friendly human? How could she leave me with this loud and bony tipper? How dare you, villain? I am **Gary the Chinchilla**, and you will pay!

Aieeeee! Owowowowow!

At last. The loud human sets me down.

Ah. Peace and stillness.

Mm. Lots of wood in here. Yum.

CHAPTER 11

WHAT MR. LURCH THOUGHT

A *little* closer to the hamster, please.

CHAPTER 12

NNNNNNNNNnnnnnnnnnnnnnnnnnnneeeeeeeeeee
eeeeeeeeeeeeeeeeeeeeeeeeeeeeeeeeeee! Zzzzzzz.
Zzzzzzz.
   Ppt!

CHAPTER 13

WHAT IGGY THOUGHT

Iggy looked around his room and felt good. Sat-isfied. Pleased with himself, his life, and his future. Over on the desk, Gary the chinchilla was squished into the farthest corner of his cage, but he wasn't *weep*-ing anymore, which meant he was okay. On the floor, in his case, Mr. Lurch was motionless, as usual. In the cage beside him, Pancake was hurling fuzz around like she expected to find hamster treasure under it. But she always did that.

Iggy was glad Ms. Schulberger had classroom pets that didn't howl or roar. Keeping a gibbon secret, now that would be hard.

A chinchilla, a hamster, and a snake were pretty good animals, Iggy decided. Not great, like a puppy. But good. And chinchillas were soft. They have the thickest fur of any land animal, he remembered.

Iggy opened the door to Gary's cage and reached in to pet the thickest fur of any land animal. *Ow.* He banged the door shut, remembering another thing about chinchillas—their teeth never stop growing, so they have to chew on things, like wood or pumice or people. Stupid chinchilla.

Still, it was just a nip, not a real bite. And his plan was still great. He lay down on his old, hairy rug and thought about it. In his mind, he imagined Sunday afternoon . . .

THE WAY IT SHOULD HAPPEN

Iggy gave his (clean) bedroom a final look. In his (clean) cage, Gary was contentedly munching a carrot. In *his* (clean) cage, Mr. Lurch was motionless. Pancake hurled a bit of fuzz onto the floor, which Iggy bent to pick up before he left the room, closing the door carefully behind him. Downstairs, in the kitchen, his mom and dad looked up as he came in. "Mom, Dad," said Iggy, "I'd like you to come upstairs and see something."

"Sure, Iggy," said his parents.

Following him upstairs, his mom joked, "I hope I'm not going to see something messy."

Iggy smiled maturely as he opened his door wide.

"What?" gasped his mom.

"Where'd you get them?" gasped his dad.

71

"They're our classroom pets. I've been taking care of them all weekend," said Iggy.

More gasping. "All weekend? We didn't hear a peep!"

"I wanted to show you that I can take care of an animal—or three—all by myself," Iggy said. "Look. They're clean and happy and well cared for."

Gary waved.

"Oooh, he's so fuzzy!" said his mom.

"Chinchillas have the thickest fur of any land animal," said Iggy. "But I still want a puppy."

His dad and his mom exchanged meaningful looks. Then they gave each other those weird little shrugs that parents give each other sometimes. "You've done a pretty good job, son," his dad admitted.

"We didn't even know they were here," said his mom.

His dad nodded. "You've shown a lot of maturity and responsibility this weekend, Iggy."

"Yes, I think you've shown us you can handle a puppy," his mom said. "Let's go to the animal shelter right now and get you one."

"Oh, no, Mom!" said Iggy quickly. "Gary and Pancake would be scared of a puppy, and they are my responsibility until tomorrow morning."

"What a mature answer, Iggy!" exclaimed his mom. "You've really proved us wrong."

"How 'bout tomorrow after school?" asked his dad. "I'll take the afternoon off."

"Sounds great!" said Iggy.

CHAPTER 14

WHAT IGGY
DIDN'T THINK

Did I latch the door to the chinchilla cage?

CHAPTER 15

THE UNINVITED

As I'm sure you're remembering, this was the night of Maribel's slumber party. Basically, that meant that, starting at six p.m., Maribel became the ruler of the house, and Iggy, his parents, and Molly had to pretend they didn't exist. While Maribel and her eight best friends ate pizza in the family room, Iggy and the rest of the family tiptoed away to eat burritos. When they tiptoed back in, the house was ringing with the joyous sounds of music, of laughter, of videos, of singing, dancing, and screeching. Was Iggy welcomed in with shouts of happiness? Was he invited to join the party and have fun?

Absolutely not.

"Time to go to your room, Ig," said his dad.

"Skedaddle," agreed his mom.

Iggy mentioned several things about being treated like a criminal even though he'd done nothing wrong. He mentioned that he was a kid, not a disease. He sighed—and bingo! He scored his dad's laptop!

Who cared about Maribel and her party? Not Iggy! In no time at all, he was lounging on his old, hairy rug watching the Nets destroy the Heat.

The Nets' forward was only ten years older than Iggy.

But he was six foot ten.

Iggy needed to grow two feet in ten years.

He was going to have to eat a lot.

Cake, for instance.

Once Iggy started thinking about cake, he couldn't stop. People are strange that way: If you want ten things and you get nine of them, that last thing—the one you don't have—becomes the thing you can't live without. Here was Iggy, all comfy in his room with a laptop full of basketball, and all he could think about was cake. Maribel had said he could have a piece of cake. But what if she forgot? What if she forgot, and she and her incredibly loud friends ate the last piece? He would get no cake!

It was a terrible thought.

He couldn't stop thinking it.

Iggy decided to go downstairs and prevent this disaster.

It would only take a minute.

He set down the laptop, rose from the floor, and slid out the door.

He did not close the door behind him.

CHAPTER 16

WHAT GARY THOUGHT

You are a fool, loud and bony human! You are a fool, and I am **Gary the Chinchilla!** You cannot contain me! You cannot imprison me! I shall escape your bony, loud self with my diabolical wit and skill.

I shall bang my head against the door— Hey! It worked!

I shall bound to freedom!

I am free! Free, free, free! Caged no more!

Good-bye, Lurch! Good-bye, little weird hamster-creature! I am off to great adventure! In this house, there is wood to chew, and I will chew it!

. . .

. . .

. . .

No, wait. I am not dead. Though I have fallen off the largest precipice in the world, I am still alive, proving once again my might and power. I am **Gary the Chinchilla**! In this house, there is wood to chew, and I will chew it!

CHAPTER 17

SURVIVAL OF THE FITTEST

Now everything was perfect. Iggy had a piece of cake and a laptop full of basketball, and the Nets were still whomping on the Heat. Everything was great.

First he ate the cake out of the frosting walls. Then he ate the frosting walls.

Yum!

He burped and noticed that Mr. Lurch was looking right at him. Was, in fact, staring at him.

It was a little bit creepy.

Did he want cake?

"You can't have cake, Mr. Lurch. You're a snake," Iggy told him.

Still, Mr. Lurch stared at him.

"Okay, just a crumb." He stood and opened the plastic hatch-door to drop a crumb into Mr. Lurch's cage.

Mr. Lurch didn't move for the crumb. He didn't even twitch. He just kept staring at Iggy.

"Well, what *do* you want, then?"

Mr. Lurch stared. It was beginning to make Iggy nervous, being stared at. "Stop it," he said.

It was kind of a relief when Pancake flew into a frenzy of senseless fuzz-hurling. Iggy dropped Mr. Lurch's hatch-door and leaned over to pick the fuzz off the floor and opened Pancake's little door to toss it back in, because he was a responsible and mature—

Suddenly, a terrible scream rang out. Actually, it was nine terrible screams, but they were all screaming the same thing:

"A RAT! A RAT! AAAAAH! RUN!"

Iggy's head jerked up. He felt a sudden sense of alarm. But why? He had done nothing wrong. Had he?

There was another shriek, a falling-from-the-top-of-the-roller-coaster shriek: "AHHHHHHHHHHHHHHHHHHHHHHHHHHHHHHH

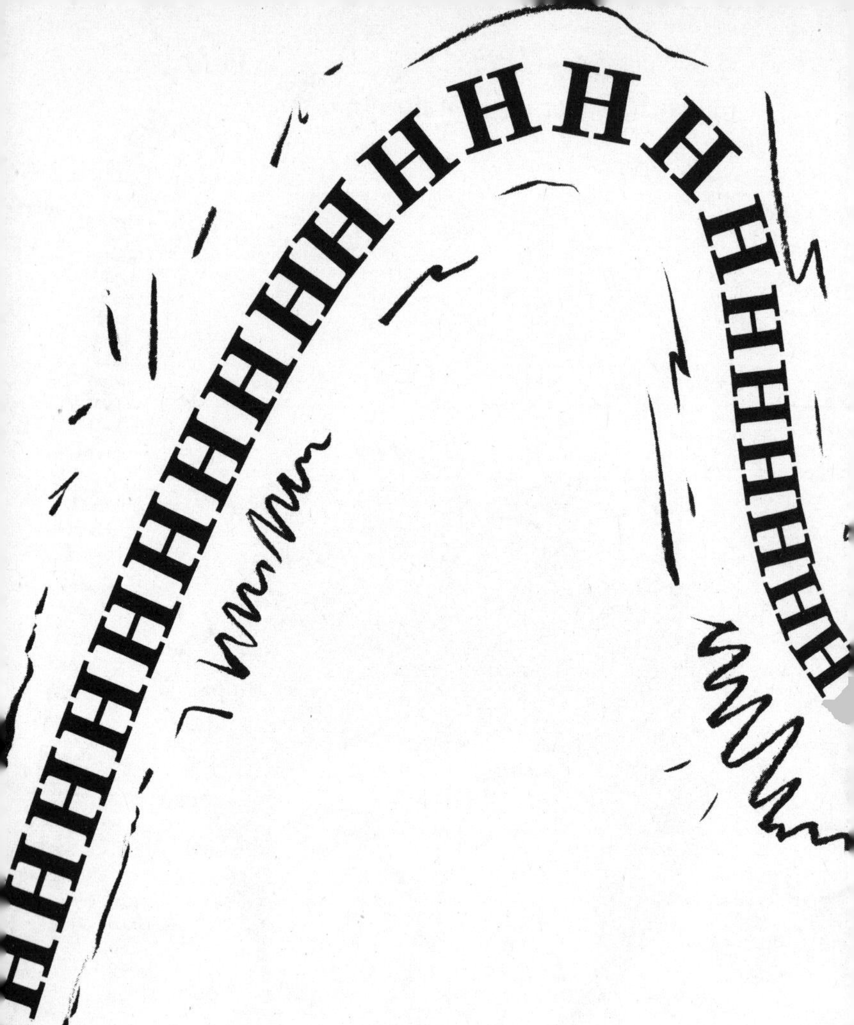

AAAAAAHHHHHHHHHHHHHHHHHHHHHHHHHHHHHHHHHHHHHHHHHHHhhhhhhhhhhhhhhhhhhhhhhhhhhhhh!"

Iggy's alarm grew. It grew into foreboding, which means "fear of doom." But why? He had done nothing wrong. Had he?

Next came yells without words in them, the sounds of running feet, slamming doors, grown-up shouts, Molly screams, more running feet, grown-ups saying bad words, and then, above it all, another scream:

"IT'S EATING THE HOUSE! IT'S A HOUSE-EATING RAT!

RUN! EVERY-ONE, RUN!"

Iggy stared at Gary's cage. The wire door was not latched. It was even slightly open.

"No," whispered Iggy, peering into the cage. *"No no no no no."*

But yes. Yes, there was no chinchilla.

"No no no," chanted Iggy.

Maybe Gary was just hiding.

Iggy swung open the door and patted hopefully inside the little hiding spot where Gary slept. He patted again. "Go ahead, bite my hand," he begged.

But there was nothing inside.

And at that moment came the most terrible
scream of all:

"CHASE IT OUTSIDE! GET IT OUT OF HERE!!"

And Iggy was off and running, running and yelling at the same time, *"NOOOO! Don't chase him outside!"*

Meanwhile, inside Iggy's room . . .

CHAPTER 18

WHAT MR. LURCH THOUGHT

So hungry.

CHAPTER 19

WHAT PANCAKE THOUGHT

NNNNNNNNNnnnnnnnnnnnnnnnnnnnnnnnnn
eeeeeeeeeeeeeeeeeeeeeeeeeeeeeeeeeeeee!

Zzzzzz. Zzzzzz.

Ppt! Ppt! Ppt!

Op! Op!

O–

CHAPTER 20

WHAT SHOULD HAVE
HAPPENED NEXT

I'm sorry to be the one to say it, but what should have happened next was what *did* happen next: Iggy got in trouble.

As you may or may not know (I'm just being polite; of course you know), there are many different kinds of trouble a kid can get in. There's the kind when your grown-ups are mad for four minutes and then start laughing. There's the kind when they yell, but mostly it's because they're worried about you (almost anytime there's blood on you, this occurs). There's the kind when they don't even yell, but their faces freeze, and you know they're really mad and you're going to be paying for it the rest of the day. Or week. Or year.

None of these was the kind of trouble Iggy was in.

Iggy was in a special kind of trouble.

It was monster-movie trouble.

It was like the part of a monster movie where the hero-person has chopped off the monster's head, and the hero-person and everyone else (including you) sighs with relief and thinks, *Whew, so much for that monster!* But while everyone's sighing, the bloody monster neck sprouts a brand-new head, and when the hero-person turns around, there's a giant open monster mouth about to eat him or her.

That's what Iggy's trouble was like: a monster sprouting new heads.

Here's how it went: In the first minutes, Iggy was only in trouble because he accidentally kicked a couple of Maribel's friends who were trying to chase Gary out of the house. But soon after that, he was in trouble for secretly keeping a chinchilla in his room. A minute or two later, he was in (a lot of) trouble for failing to latch Gary's cage. In the following minute, he was in trouble because Gary bit Iggy's dad while he was carrying him back to Iggy's room.

Then, once Iggy's dad saw Iggy's room, Iggy was in trouble for secretly keeping not only a chinchilla but also a snake and a hamster in his room. A few seconds later, he was in trouble because the snake and the hamster were missing, owing to the fact that Iggy had failed to latch *any* of the animal cages in his room. Not long after that, he was in trouble because the snake turned up. The snake in turn caused three of Maribel's friends to scream, and Iggy was in trouble for that too. Immediately afterward, he was in trouble because he was too scared of Mr. Lurch to pick him up.

There was a short break in Iggy's trouble when Maribel's friend Kate turned out to like snakes, and she picked Mr. Lurch up and put him back in his cage. Unfortunately for Iggy, when picking him up, Kate discovered that Mr. Lurch had just eaten, and very soon after *that*, it became clear that what he had eaten was Pancake.

At this point, everyone stared at Iggy in hatred and disgust, which was really the worst part.

Then two of Maribel's friends started crying about Pancake, and Iggy got in trouble for (a) that and (b) ruining Maribel's party. That was a bad part too.

It was followed by a period when everyone was supposed

to settle down and go to sleep, and Iggy found that he *couldn't* go to sleep because chinchillas run around all night with their toenails scrabbling. Plus, he felt bad about Pancake. And about Ms. Schulberger, who had trusted him. Also, Mr. Lurch was creeping him out.

Not long after that, Iggy got in trouble for moving Mr. Lurch's cage into the hall.

The next morning, it seemed as though he was in trouble simply for being alive, but this soon morphed into being in trouble for not having $17.95, which was the price of a new hamster. After agreeing to no allowance for five weeks, Iggy went with his dad to the pet store and got a hamster. When he arrived home, Iggy put the new hamster into Pancake's freshly cleaned cage; checked all the latches of all the cages about twenty times; and dropped down on his old, hairy rug, breathing a sigh of relief.

And just like the relieved hero-person in the monster movie, there was more trouble coming his way.

"Iggy," he heard. "Come down here, please. We need to have a talk."

CHAPTER 21

A
VERY EDUCATIONAL
CHAPTER
CONTAINING
A READING QUIZ

I bet that at some point in your life you've had the kind of talk Iggy then had with his parents. Actually, I bet you've had more than one. I bet you'd get an A if you took a test on it. Let's see:

The following sentence openers occurred in

the talk Iggy's parents had with him. Pick the most likely ending to the sentence.

1. "Your father and I are . . ."
   a. thinking about moving to Omaha, Nebraska. Would you like to come too?
   b. very disappointed in you.
   c. kittens.

2. "After you apologize to Maribel for ruining her party . . ."
   a. you can have an ice cream.
   b. you will have completed your punishment.
   c. you will write a letter to Ms. Schulberger explaining what happened and apologizing for your carelessness. You'll have plenty of time to make it perfect, because you're going to be in your room until dinnertime. Furthermore, there will be no video games or TV whatsoever for a week, and we don't want to hear any complaining on that topic.

3. "And most of all, Iggy, we want you to understand that you have demonstrated to us that . . ."

  a. you're afraid of snakes.

  b. you're only a kid.

  c. you are not nearly responsible and mature enough to take care of *any* animal, much less a puppy. We know you've got your heart set on having a dog, and we're sorry to have to say that you will *not* be getting a puppy in the near future.*

---

*Answers: b, c. Did you get them all right? Cool! See how educational it is to get in trouble?

CHAPTER 22

WHAT SHOULDN'T HAVE HAPPENED NEXT BUT DID, BECAUSE IGGY WAS BY THIS TIME COMPLETELY SICK OF ANIMALS, ALL ANIMALS

Iggy was glad.*

---

*For a while.

Even though **ANNIE BARROWS** is (very) mature and responsible, she has no pets. Why, you ask? Because one time she babysat a hamster, and it died. Two months later, the same people asked her to babysit their new hamster. Guess what. It died too! If you would like her to babysit *your* hamster, email annie@anniebarrows.com.

PS: She didn't do anything to them. They just died.

anniebarrows.com
@anniebarrowsauthor

SAM RICKS is the illustrator of the Geisel Award winner *Don't Throw It to Mo!* and the Stinkbomb and Ketchup-Face books. He is grateful his parents let him live through a surprising number of Iggycidents. Sam lives with his family in Utah.

samricks.com
@samuelricks

READ ABOUT ALL OF
IGGY'S TRIUMPHS!